Troublesome Trucks

Based on
The Railway Series
by the
Rev. W. Awdry

Illustrations by
Robin Davies
and **Nigel Chilvers**

DEAN

This edition published 2019 by Dean, an imprint of Egmont UK Limited,
The Yellow Building, 1 Nicholas Road, London W11 4AN

Thomas the Tank Engine & Friends ™

HiT entertainment

ISBN 978 0 6035 7724 6
70608/001
Printed in Italy

Written by Emily Stead. Designed by Claire Yeo.
Series designed by Martin Aggett.

The first time I worked with
the Troublesome Trucks, they
were tricky to handle. I didn't
listen to Edward when he tried
to tell me how much mischief
they could cause . . .

Thomas was tired of pulling coaches.

"I want to try something new!" he would tell his friends in the Sheds each night.

The other engines didn't take much notice. They knew Thomas had a lot to learn.

One night, Edward said kindly, "Why don't you take my trucks tomorrow and I'll pull your coaches?"

"Oh, thank you, Edward!" Thomas smiled.

Edward warned Thomas that trucks were **silly, noisy** things that loved to play tricks on engines, but Thomas was too excited to listen.

The next morning, Thomas coupled up to Edward's trucks. But they didn't want to go.

"Come on, come on," Thomas puffed, giving the trucks a hard little **bump.**

"Ouch!" they cried, as Thomas pulled them onto the Main Line.

Thomas was happy to be doing something new. "Come along, come along," he sang.

"All right, all right," the trucks grumbled.

They **clattered** through stations and **rumbled** over bridges. The trucks didn't like being **bumped,** and waited for a chance to cause trouble.

Thomas soon reached the top of Gordon's Hill.

"Steady," warned his Driver, as he shut off the steam.

Thomas puffed to a stop.

"No! No!" said the trucks, naughtily. "Go on! Go on!"

Then, with an enormous **shove,** they pushed Thomas down the hill!

Thomas raced down the steep hill at full speed. The trucks **rattled** and **giggled** behind him.

"Stop pushing!" Thomas wheeshed, but the trucks would not stop.

"Huff, huff, ho! You're too slow.
We'll give you a push to help you go!" they sang.

Thomas could see the station at the bottom of the hill, but he was going too fast to stop.

"Cinders and ashes!" he cried.

He whooshed straight past the platform. Everyone was surprised to see Thomas pulling a train of trucks, and going so fast, too.

At the points, the line split into two tracks. Thomas turned off the Main Line and into a goods yard.

"Oh dear! Oh dear!" Thomas moaned. His axles **tingled,** as he **skidded** along the rails.

He was heading straight for the buffers at the end of the track. Thomas was going to crash!

His Driver applied the brakes even harder,
as they rolled closer and closer to the buffers.
Thomas shut his eyes.

But there was no crash.

Thomas opened one eye carefully. He had
stopped just in front of the buffers! But next to
the track was The Fat Controller, looking very
cross.

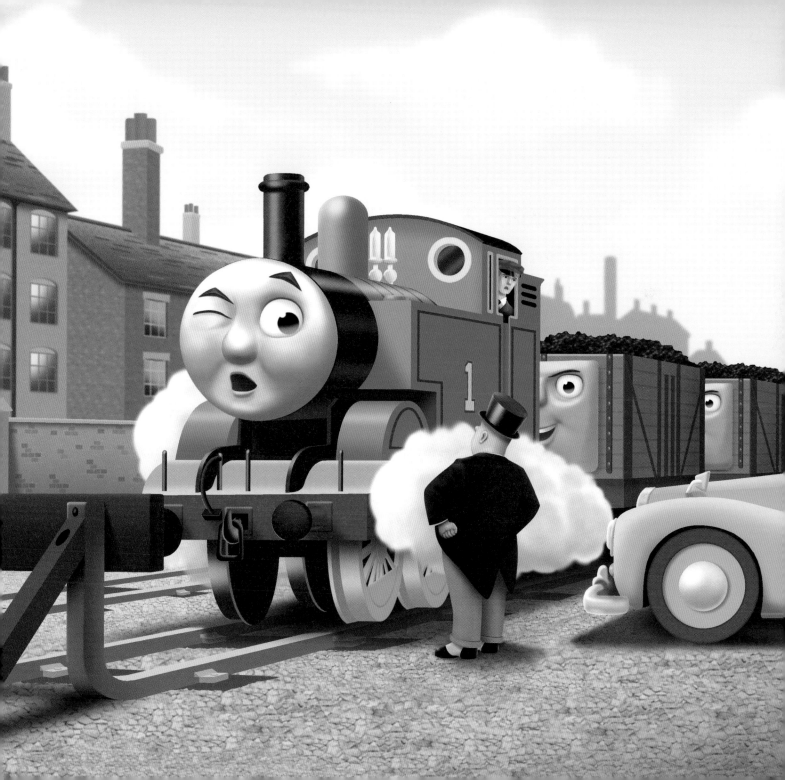

"Why did you come in so fast, Thomas?"
The Fat Controller boomed.

"The trucks pushed me," Thomas said sadly.

"You must learn to make trucks behave,"
The Fat Controller told him. "Only then will
you be a **Really Useful Engine.**"

"Yes, Sir!" Thomas promised.

The next day, Edward showed Thomas how to pull the trucks properly, and keep them in line when they played their naughty tricks.

Thomas stopped bumping them . . . except when they didn't behave.

From that day, Thomas never complained about his coaches again. They were much easier to pull than those Troublesome Trucks!

More about the trucks

wooden sides

buffer

coupling hook

Thomas' challenge to you

Look back through the pages of this book
and see if you can spot:

Bertie

passengers

oil drum

moon

cows

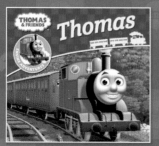
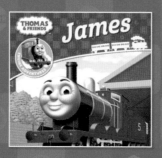

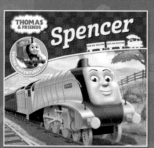
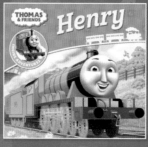
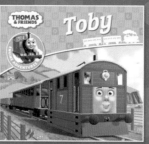

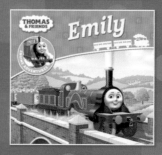